Where is

by Michèle Dufresne

Pioneer Valley Educational Press, Inc.

Here is Peanut.

Peanut is a guinea pig.

3

Here is Laura.
Peanut is Laura's guinea pig.
Laura likes to play
with Peanut.

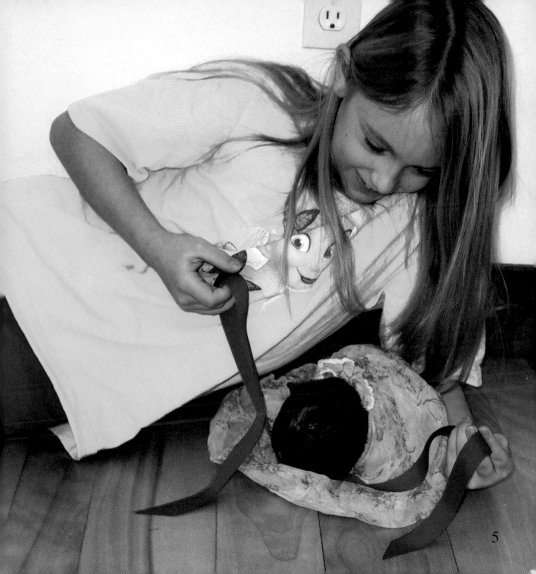

"Oh, no!" said Laura. "Where is Peanut?"

"Peanut! Peanut!"
said Laura.
"Where are you Peanut?"
Laura looked and looked
for Peanut.
"Peanut! Peanut!
Where are you?"

9

Mom looked for Peanut.
Mom looked and looked
and looked.
"Peanut! Peanut!
Where are you, Peanut?"

11

"Oh, look!" said Laura.
"Here is Peanut!"

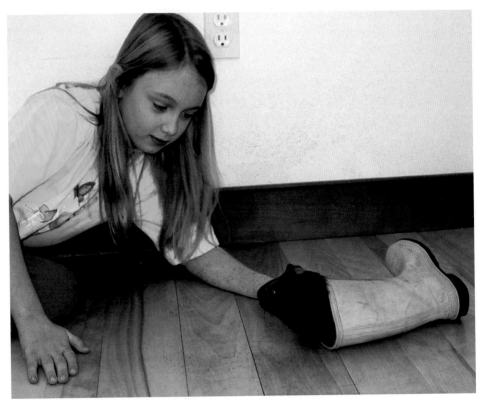